A CHAMPIONSHIP ON THE LINE

"This is a mystery," he said, "at the worst possible time. I've lost my lucky necklace right before Game 7, when I'm going to need all the luck I can get."

Zoe stepped behind their dad and Uncle Marty, and motioned for Zach to join her. She didn't want Mike Gordon to see the smile she could feel spreading across her face, without any way of stopping it. She wasn't happy that he'd lost his necklace, of course. She knew this was serious to him, and how important that necklace was. It was almost as if it had magic powers.

But Mike "Boston" Gordon had just said the magic word for her:

Mystery.

And considering the stakes—Game 7 of the Stanley Cup finals—it might be the biggest mystery the Walker twins ever had to solve.

D0041506

ALSO BY #1 BESTSELLER MIKE LUPICA

Travel Team

Heat

Miracle on 49th Street

Summer Ball

The Big Field

Million-Dollar Throw

The Batboy

Hero

The Underdogs

True Legend

QB 1

Fantasy League

Fast Break

Last Man Out

Lone Stars

Shoot-Out

No Slam Dunk

Strike Zone

THE ZACH & ZOE MYSTERIES:

The Missing Baseball

The Half-Court Hero

The Football Fiasco

The Soccer Secret

THE ZACH & ZOE MYSTERIES
THE HOCKEY RINK HUNT

Mike Lupica

illustrated by
Chris Danger

WITHDRAWN

Puffin Books

PUFFIN BOOKS
An imprint of Penguin Random House LLC, New York

Published simultaneously by Puffin Books and Philomel Books,
imprints of Penguin Random House LLC, 2019

Text copyright © 2019 by Mike Lupica
Illustrations copyright © 2019 by Chris Danger

Penguin supports copyright. Copyright fuels creativity, encourages diverse voices, promotes free speech, and creates a vibrant culture. Thank you for buying an authorized edition of this book and for complying with copyright laws by not reproducing, scanning, or distributing any part of it in any form without permission. You are supporting writers and allowing Penguin to continue to publish books for every reader.

VISIT US ONLINE AT PENGUINRANDOMHOUSE.COM

LIBRARY OF CONGRESS CATALOGING-IN-PUBLICATION DATA IS AVAILABLE.

ISBN: 9780425289495

Printed in the United States of America

3 5 7 9 10 8 6 4 2

Design by Maria Fazio
Illustrations by Chris Danger
Text set in Fournier MT Std

This is a work of fiction. Names, characters, places, and incidents either are the product of the author's imagination or are used fictitiously, and any resemblance to actual persons, living or dead, businesses, companies, events, or locales is entirely coincidental.

Once again, for Taylor McKelvy Lupica

ONE

If there was one thing the Walker twins, Zach and Zoe, loved almost as much as a mystery, it was a surprise. And suddenly, their afternoon was about to be full of them.

First, their grandpa Richie showed up unexpectedly at their house after they got home from Middletown Elementary.

Zach and Zoe had known Grandpa Richie was coming over for dinner, but usually he didn't show up until later in the evening. He lived in their neighborhood, and often walked from his house to Zach and Zoe's.

When Zoe asked why he was early today, her grandfather gave her a wink.

"I heard there might be something interesting brewin' at your house today," he said.

"Like what?" Zach said, furrowing his brow.

"Well, how about a game of two-on-two basketball for starters?" Grandpa Richie said.

"There's only three of us here," Zoe pointed out, "unless you can convince Mom to play. But she's already inside getting dinner started."

Now Grandpa Richie raised his eyebrows and grinned. It seemed like he was hiding something from them. As if he knew something the twins didn't.

"Are you two sure there are only three of us?" he said.

"Grandpa!" Zoe said. "You're acting mysterious."

"And who better to do that with than my grandchildren?" he said.

"Okay," said Zach, "what do you know that we don't?"

"A lot!" Grandpa Richie teased, and they all laughed. "Don't I always tell you that with age comes wisdom?"

"All the time," Zoe said. "Now please will you tell us the wisdom you're holding back from us right now?"

"It's not so much wisdom as a surprise," he said, looking down at his watch. "A surprise that I believe should be pulling into your driveway any minute now."

It actually took about five more minutes. But then their dad's car pulled up to the house. He'd come home early from his job at the television station, which was unusual.

Zoe and her brother ran to the driver's side door to greet their dad. "What are you doing here?" Zoe asked, now more confused than ever.

"Well," Danny Walker said, "I heard a rumor that my kids and their grandfather might need a fourth for a game of two-on-two."

Now he was the one winking, at Grandpa Richie.

"What I meant to say," Danny said, "is that I heard there might be a game brewin' here today."

The twins looked at each other, puzzled. There was that word again: brewin'. But all they really cared about in that moment was the game they were about to play in their driveway.

"So you and Grandpa Richie showing up for a game is our surprise?" Zach asked.

"It's a surprise," his dad said. "Just not the best one you might get today."

"But the next surprise is one the two of you are going to have to earn," Grandpa Richie added.

"Tell us how," Zoe said. "You know Zach and I love challenges, too."

"You have to win the game we're about to play to find out more," Grandpa Richie said. "The two of you against your dad and me."

The twins' smiles turned into frowns at the exact same time.

"Wait a second!" Zach said. "Those sides aren't fair. We never play grown-ups versus twins."

Danny Walker looked at Grandpa Richie now, as if *he* was the one who was confused.

"Not fair?" he said, shrugging his shoulders.

"I heard the same thing you did," Grandpa Richie said. "But seems to me that one of the guys on our team is an old man."

"You're not old!" the twins said together. It was something they often said to their grandfather, usually in one voice.

"I don't see any problem with the teams," Danny Walker said.

"We may be younger," Zoe said. "But you two are bigger."

Now the twins saw a big smile appear on their dad's face. Their mom, Tess, called it his Christmas morning smile. He looked as young and happy as his eight-year-old twins.

"Glad you brought that up, Zoe," he said. "What am I always telling you and your brother about sports and size?"

Zoe looked at Zach. He looked at her. They smiled because they both knew what their dad was thinking. It was just like in school when their teachers called on them, and they knew the right answer.

"It's not the size of the player that matters," Zoe started.

"It's the size of their talent," Zach continued for her.

"And the size of their heart," Zoe finished.

"That's what I always told your dad," Grandpa Richie said, "back when he was a boy. He was the smallest one in just about every basketball game he ever played."

"So," their dad said, "how about one of you grabs the basketball in the garage and we get this party started?"

While Zach ran to get the ball, Zoe turned to their dad.

"You still haven't told us what we'd win," she said.

"First, let's see if you *can* win," said Danny.

He hurried inside to change into his sneakers. Grandpa Richie already had his on. The twins couldn't remember a time when their grandpa wasn't wearing sneakers. He had been a basketball star once, and made it all the way to the NBA before getting injured. His son, the twins' father, had also played professionally. Grandpa Richie loved telling his grandchildren that he still felt like the boy in the old basketball pictures they loved going through.

They all decided it would be a game of ten baskets. Zach guarded his dad. Zoe guarded

Grandpa Richie. As usual when it was the four of them in the driveway like this, there was a lot of good passing. The twins had been taught by both their father and grandfather that everything in basketball began with a good pass.

They were also told that if you played hard and had fun, you couldn't lose. Not really. But the twins didn't want to lose this particular game, because there was some kind of prize waiting for them if they won. They didn't know exactly what it was, but they couldn't wait to find out.

Grandpa Richie and Danny Walker were playing their hardest, and still having a ton of fun. But even though they were bigger, the twins were faster. Zoe went flying past Grandpa Richie for an easy layup during one play. He bent over to put his hands on his knees and laughed. "Slow down!" he called.

Zoe laughed, too.

"Now, that's something neither of you ever taught us to do," Zoe said.

Slightly out of breath, Grandpa Richie said to Danny, "Where'd they get these moves?"

"Well, I'd like to say they got 'em from us," he said. "But I'm seeing moves from both of them today that I don't even recognize."

Finally the game was tied at 9–9. Zach was on the outside, dribbling the ball. But as he looked over at his sister, he gave her the slightest nod of his head. Zoe knew what he wanted her to do. They read each other's minds a lot. It was like they were sharing the same brain.

Zoe faked to the outside, toward Zach. When Grandpa Richie fell for the fake, thinking he might steal a pass, Zoe immediately cut for the basket. Zach threw a perfect bounce pass to his sister, who caught it in stride. Then Zoe made the layup that won them the game.

Zach ran for his sister, so they could do their favorite Zach-and-Zoe celebration: the special high five they invented. They jumped and spun around and bumped hips and elbows, as if it were a dance routine only they knew.

When they were finished, Zoe looked at their dad, hands on her hips.

"Okay," she said, "now that we've won, you have to tell us *what* we've won."

"Yeah," said Zach. "What's the surprise?"

Danny turned to face the twins. "Actually, there are two surprises. Dad, why don't you tell them the first one?" he said, turning to Grandpa Richie.

Grandpa Richie's eyes twinkled as he smiled at his grandkids, sensing their excitement.

"Okay, here it goes. Your parents are taking you to Game 7 of the Stanley Cup finals in Boston two nights from now."

"No way!" Zoe shouted.

"Way," their grandfather said.

"But before we go to the game," Danny cut in, "I have to interview a bunch of players at the Bruins' practice tomorrow. I've arranged for you both to come with me into the locker room."

"No way!" Zoe said again. "We hardly ever get to go with you when you're working."

"Hey," their dad said, "the two of you earned it."

"Told you something was brewin'," Grandpa Richie said to the Walker twins. "Just didn't tell you it was the Boston Bruins."

TWO

The Bruins' practice facility was right off the highway toward downtown Boston. When Zach and Zoe saw the name outside the place they almost couldn't believe it.

"The Warrior Ice Arena!" Zoe exclaimed. "How perfect is that?"

A long time ago, Grandpa Richie had played with the Golden State Warriors in the NBA. It was why Danny Walker had nicknamed his old travel team the Warriors. And that was why the

Walker twins had named one of their summer-league basketball teams the Warriors.

"It's almost as if we were supposed to end up here today," Zach said to their dad.

"There are lots of cool stories in our family attached to that name," Danny Walker said. "Now we've got the chance to write another one today."

Little did they know at the time just how much of a story it would turn out to be.

Once the twins and their dad were inside, they watched the Bruins practice. They walked up close to the ice and peered through the glass partition. Neither Zach nor Zoe could believe how exciting hockey was up close. They were passing and cutting and shooting the puck and somehow coming to complete stops no matter how fast they were going. It was even more impressive that they were doing it all on ice skates!

"And we think *we're* fast," Zoe joked to her brother.

"This is a little different from what we used to do at Twin Rinks," Zach replied.

Twin Rinks was the skating facility back in Middletown where they'd first learned to skate.

When the Bruins' practice came to an end, the players returned to the locker room. Tons of reporters and media people followed to get their interviews. But after a few minutes had gone by, a tall, bearded man came up to Danny. He introduced himself to the twins as Mr. Greenberg, the assistant general manager of the team. Mr. Greenberg, as it turned out, was a friend of their dad's from Middletown High School. He escorted Danny and the twins down the hall toward the locker room.

By the time Zach, Zoe, and their dad got to the locker room entrance, most of the Bruins players had showered and were changing into their regular clothes. The twins waited outside for them to get dressed while Mr. Greenberg told them about the Stanley Cup finals so far. The Bruins and the San Jose Sharks had battled it out on the ice for six exciting games.

The teams were gearing up for Game 7, which was to be played the following night at Boston's TD Garden. Zach and Zoe had attended a couple of Boston Celtics basketball games at the Garden with their dad, but they had never seen a hockey game in person.

Now they weren't just going to see their first live game, they were also going to see the winner of the game awarded the Stanley Cup. Their dad explained it wasn't just the oldest trophy in team sports in North America, but perhaps the most famous, too.

Danny Walker's cameraman, Marty Pearl, whom the twins called Uncle Marty, was waiting for them when they got inside the locker room. Zach and Zoe walked in with their dad and looked around in wonder. The locker room seemed almost as big as the hockey rink! Uncle Marty was standing next to the locker of the Bruins' biggest star, Mike Gordon. The twins knew Mike's nickname was "Boston"

Gordon, because of the arena in which the Bruins played. Two nights ago, it had been Mike's goal in the last seconds of Game 6 that had evened the finals at three games all.

Mike Gordon didn't look that much older than the teenager he'd been when he first started playing for the Bruins. But Zach and Zoe both knew enough about hockey to know that Mike wasn't just the Bruins' best player, he was one of the best hockey players in the world.

As soon as Danny had introduced Zach and Zoe to Mike, they could all tell something was wrong. And that seemed wrong to the Walker twins. After all, Mike had just scored the biggest goal of his life at the end of Game 6. Not only that, he was getting ready to play the biggest game of his life tomorrow night.

Mike was polite and friendly enough, answering all of Danny Walker's questions once Uncle Marty's camera was rolling. But when the interview was over and the camera lights had been turned off, their dad said to Mike, "May I ask you one more question?"

"Sure," Mike said. "You know I always enjoy talking to you."

"Is something bothering you today?" Danny asked.

"Actually, there is," Mike Gordon said. "I don't want you or the twins to think what I'm about to tell you is silly. But right before you came in here, I realized that I'd lost my lucky necklace."

He told them it was a simple gold necklace his parents had given him before his first game with the Bruins. Later on, his wife added a locket to it. Inside the locket was a picture of her and their two small children.

"The locket completes the necklace. Just like my wife and kids do for me," he said. "I wear it under my jersey, but it makes me feel connected to my family, even when I'm on the ice. I've never played a single game in my National

Hockey League career without it around my neck."

"I don't think it's silly at all," Zoe said. "Pretty much everybody I know believes in good-luck charms."

"One time we got to a baseball game," Zach said, "and I couldn't find the lucky silver dollar my grandpa Richie had given me. I almost asked my mom to go home to see if she could find it before the game started."

"Until I found it for you," Zoe chimed in. "It was in your bag and had fallen into your glove."

Zach nodded. "My sister is good at finding things," he said to Mike.

"I just don't know what could have happened to it," Mike said about the necklace. "I was about to put on my shirt after my shower, and I reached up out of habit to touch the necklace, but it was gone. I looked through my locker and my gear and even around the lockers next to mine. But somehow it's disappeared."

He shook his head.

"This is a mystery," he said, "at the worst possible time. I've lost my lucky necklace right before Game 7, when I'm going to need all the luck I can get."

Zoe stepped behind their dad and Uncle Marty, and motioned for Zach to join her. She didn't want Mike Gordon to see the smile she could feel spreading across her face, without any way of stopping it. She wasn't happy that he'd lost his necklace, of course. She knew this was serious to him, and how important that necklace was. It was almost as if it had magic powers.

But Mike "Boston" Gordon had just said the magic word for her:

Mystery.

And considering the stakes—Game 7 of the Stanley Cup finals—it might be the biggest mystery the Walker twins ever had to solve.

THREE

Zach always admired Zoe for her confidence, whether in school, in sports, or especially in mysteries. He could see that confidence now, even standing in front of a famous athlete's locker. Zach loved solving mysteries as much as Zoe, but Zoe always took her excitement to the next level.

Zoe stepped back in front of Mike Gordon. "Maybe we can help," she said.

Mike grinned as if he couldn't help himself.

Maybe he was seeing the same confidence Zach had always seen in his sister. She did appear pretty fearless the way she'd stepped up and offered to help.

"You think you can find my lucky necklace the way you found your brother's silver dollar?" he asked, sounding hopeful.

Zach smiled and reached into his pocket. He pulled out the silver dollar to show Mike.

"Still got it," he said. "Maybe it will help bring us luck to find your necklace."

"When it comes to solving mysteries," Danny Walker said to Mike, "my kids are the all-stars."

Then Zoe said to Mike, "Do you have time to answer a couple more questions?"

"If it will help find my necklace," Mike said, "I'll be even happier to answer your questions than I was your dad's."

"Could you go through everything you did once practice was over?" Zoe said. She didn't have a notebook to write everything down, but her memory worked just as well.

Mike looked over at Danny Walker.

"Your daughter sounds as if she might have a job like yours someday," he said.

"Maybe by the time she's ten," Danny replied with a grin.

Mike turned back to Zoe then. "You really think this will help?"

Zoe shrugged and smiled. "How much time was left in Game 6 when you scored that goal?" she said.

"Twenty seconds," said Mike.

"You didn't give up, and neither will we," Zach said.

Mike told them that once practice ended, he came straight to his locker. Then he got out of his gear and took a shower, and that's when he realized the necklace was gone. He said he even went back and checked the shower room and the area next to it with sinks and mirrors for the players.

"Is that all?" Zoe said. "Is it possible you may have forgotten something you did?"

"Honestly?" Mike said. "It's definitely possible. All I'd been thinking about was Game 7, at least until I realized my necklace had gone missing."

"Could you have taken it off without real-izing it?" Zach asked.

Mike shook his head.

"Never," he said. "That I *would* remember."

"You do have an awful lot on your mind today," Zoe said.

"My brain is filled with a million thoughts about Game 7. I want to win it so badly for my teammates, for Boston, for myself," he said.

"And you said you already checked around your locker, right?" Zach said.

"I did," he said. "It's not here. I went through my jersey and T-shirt, even looked inside my skates." He shook his head again, his face sad. "Somehow I've lost my own lucky charm before I play for the biggest prize in hockey."

"We're going to find it for you," Zoe Walker said, determined.

"You did something nice for us by letting us meet you today," Zach said. "It's only right we do something nice for you."

"Wow," Mike said. "I know I'm feeling the pressure of Game 7 tomorrow night. But it sounds like you're the ones putting pressure on yourselves now."

"They sort of thrive on it," Danny Walker said. "Even at eight years old."

Some Bruins players were still in front of their lockers. A few were out on the ice for some last minute practice before the big game. Mike took Zach and Zoe into the middle of the room and introduced them as his brand-new friends.

"These are the world's youngest detectives! They're on the case, looking for my missing necklace," he said.

"You've got to find it," said Joe Craig, the right winger on Mike's line. "He wasn't even this upset when he accidentally broke his stick in the middle of Game 3!"

The locker to the right of Mike's was empty by now. Zach asked if it was all right for him and his sister to check around in there, even though Mike said he already had.

Mike said it was fine with him. The twins checked around, thoroughly. The necklace wasn't there.

Alex Mozov, the left winger on Mike's line, happened to have the locker to Mike's left. Alex gave a thorough search of his own locker, but also came up empty.

"It has to be here somewhere," Mike said.

"And my brother and I are going to find out where," Zoe said with certainty.

"It's not going to be easy," said Mike.

Zoe smiled at him. "But it's like one of the announcers said after you scored that goal in Game 6. If what you did against the Sharks was easy, everybody would do it."

"We're not trying to win Game 7 for you," Zach said. "Only you and your teammates can do that. But we *are* sort of trying to get an assist."

FOUR

The last few Bruins who stayed on the ice finally came inside the locker room.

"They're like us when we're playing outside and don't want to come in for dinner," Zoe remarked. "They know their season is over tomorrow night, but don't want to stop playing."

"I've learned so much just by being here," Zach said.

"Including how star athletes are just as superstitious as anybody else," Zoe said.

"It's more than that," her brother said. "Even though these players are some of the best in the world, they still love sports the same way we do."

Their dad came over then, having overheard their conversation. "It's just like Grandpa Richie says: the boy in him never really left," he said.

Danny still had one more player to interview before the head coach: the Bruins goalie, Jeff Costello, who had just made his way into the locker room. He walked over to Jeff's locker, and Uncle Marty handed him his microphone before turning on the camera light. Danny asked Jeff a few questions about Game 7, and before long it was time for Jeff to hit the showers. So Danny, Uncle Marty, Zach, and Zoe had to leave the locker room, at least for the time being.

Danny headed to the coach's office for his final interview. The coach had called a meeting with the assistant coaches after practice ended, and it was just letting out. The twins couldn't believe how much was still going on, even though practice was over. They could only imagine what it was like for everybody on a game day.

Their dad told Zach and Zoe to head toward the rink and he'd meet them there once his interview was over. Zach and Zoe walked up to the ice and noticed the man who drove the Zamboni getting ready to start it up. The Zamboni drove up and down the rink to resurface and smooth the ice. In an hour, people would be skating around on the same ice the Bruins had just used.

"That Zamboni reminds me of a giant lawn mower," said Zach. "Only instead of cutting grass, it smooths the ice on a hockey rink."

His sister barely heard him.

She was staring at the Zamboni.

"Wait a second," she said.

Zach turned and saw an expression on her face he recognized. It was one he'd seen plenty of times before. Right away he knew she'd noticed something, or had an idea she thought might help them find Mike Gordon's missing necklace.

"Go ask Dad if we can ride along on the Zamboni," Zoe said. "I'm going to ask the driver the same thing. If Mike's necklace somehow fell off during practice, we don't want the machine to run over it."

"On it," her brother said, and took off down the hallway at full speed for the coach's office. Zoe ran over to the glass near the ice and waved to get the Zamboni driver's attention. When he saw her, he smiled and got down from behind the wheel. Slowly, he walked over to where Zoe was standing, careful not to slip on the ice.

"You're one of Danny Walker's kids, right?" the man said, introducing himself as Mr. Doherty.

"Yes sir," she said. "I'm Zoe. My brother Zach just went to ask our dad if we could ride along with you . . . if that's okay."

"And why would you want to do that?" Mr. Doherty asked.

As quickly as she could, she explained about Mike Gordon's missing necklace, and how important it was to him. "He's never played a game without it," she said, "and definitely not one as big as Game 7."

While she was doing her best to convince Mr. Doherty to let them ride along, she saw Zach running back down the hallway. He was giving her a thumbs-up, which meant he'd gotten permission from their dad.

"I'd do anything for Mike," Mr. Doherty said after Zoe introduced him to Zach. "He's an even better person than he is a hockey player, which is saying something."

"So we can ride along?" Zoe asked, hopeful.

"What are we waiting for?" Mr. Doherty said with a smile.

They went over to the Bruins bench and hopped over the boards, just the way the players did. Then Mr. Doherty took them both by the arms so they wouldn't slip on the ice, and helped them into the seat next to him.

"I usually go pretty slow in this thing," he said. "But I'm thinking we should go even slower today. I feel as if we might be looking for a needle in a haystack."

"I think my sister could even spot one of those," Zach said.

As Mr. Doherty drove the Zamboni, he leaned out from behind the wheel so he could study the ice in front of him more closely. Zach and Zoe did the same from where they were sitting. It wasn't just Zoe who had great vision. Zach prided himself on his own vision, too, especially when it came to sports.

But none of them spotted the necklace on the ice. By the time Mr. Doherty had gone up and back across the rink, they were convinced

Mike hadn't dropped his necklace on the ice after all.

It was somewhere in this arena, it just had to be. But it wasn't out here in the rink.

"We've got to find that necklace," Zoe said, sounding more determined than ever. "Mike is our friend now, and he needs that necklace for the game tomorrow."

"Which means he needs us," Zach said.

They thanked Mr. Doherty for the ride, and he wished them luck. Then they stepped off the Zamboni and walked off the ice. Their dad would be finished working soon, but it seemed their own work was just beginning.

Mike's big game was tomorrow night at the Garden. But Zach and Zoe's was right here, right now.

FIVE

Zach and Zoe waited near the ice for their dad, who was just finishing his interview with the Bruins coach. Now he and Uncle Marty were heading toward the rink, ready to set up the camera near the ice.

The twins knew this was where their dad would speak directly into the camera and put what he called a "tag" on his piece.

"The tag," Danny Walker had explained to them once, "is like what you do when you sum up a paper you've written for school."

It was what viewers at home would watch after Danny's interviews with the players had aired on TV. Kind of like a roundup.

He told the twins that he wouldn't be long, and he'd meet them back at the locker room door in twenty minutes. Zach and Zoe took another walk back down the hallway, passing an open door where they heard a man talking on the telephone.

The door read SECURITY, so Zach and Zoe were careful not to intrude. On their way to the practice that morning, their dad explained that it wasn't just the Bruins who used the Warrior Ice Arena. Sometimes the youth hockey teams played their games there, too. Many also came for skating lessons, or just to have a free skate on the smooth ice Mr. Doherty's Zamboni machine made.

They stopped outside the office as they heard the man inside say, "Well, I can't make any promises about your son's sweater, ma'am. But I'll certainly check the Lost and Found for you."

Zoe turned to Zach. He could see the excitement on her face.

"Why didn't we think of that?" she said, slapping a palm to her forehead. "Somebody might already have found the necklace and put it in the Lost and Found! They wouldn't have known it was Mike's."

They waited patiently for the man to finish his phone call. When he did, they knocked on the open door, and the security guard invited them in. Zach and Zoe introduced themselves quickly, but were eager to explain about the missing necklace.

"How can I help you kids today?" the security guard said. His nametag read MR. AMARO and he wore a big, friendly smile on his face.

"Mike Gordon lost his lucky necklace and we're trying to help him find it," Zach began. "My sister and I overheard you on the phone saying something about a Lost and F—"

Mr. Amaro chuckled, and jumped up from behind his desk and grabbed his keys before

Zach could even finish his sentence.

"C'mon!" he said, waving a hand at Zach and Zoe to follow him. "I'll do anything to help the Bruins. They've been my favorite team since I was your age."

Mr. Amaro said he had to get back to work soon. But he offered to walk them down to the Lost and Found and then find their dad to let him know where they were.

"But I've got to warn you," he said. "There's a lot of stuff in that room. You can't believe the things people leave behind in this place."

"We're not afraid of hard work," Zach said.

Mr. Amaro grinned. "I could tell that as soon as the two of you came through my door," he said. "Looks as if the whole Walker family is working here today."

He hadn't been kidding about the amount of stuff in the Lost and Found. The twins were surprised it all fit into one room.

"We'll never be able to go through all of this before we have to leave," Zach said.

"So we'll do as much as we can until we have to meet Dad," Zoe said.

"I feel like Mike must have felt at the end of Game 6 with the clock winding down," Zach said as he scanned the room.

"But he found what he needed that night," Zoe reminded him. "The winning goal!"

They got to work. Zach took one side of the room, Zoe took the other. There were so many articles of clothing lying around: sweaters and T-shirts and windbreakers and a few pairs of sneakers. They even found a parka that must have been there since last winter. There were umbrellas and old hockey pucks and sticks and skate guards.

There was pretty much everything except a gold necklace with a locket attached to it.

"Hey," Zach said from his side of the room. "Look at this!"

He held up a shoe for his sister to see. It must have belonged to a grown-up, because it was too big to be a kid's size. "Someone lost one shoe! How is that even possible?"

Zach giggled thinking about how it would look if someone were leaving the arena with only one shoe on. Zoe looked up at the shoe Zach was holding and immediately stopped what she was doing.

"Look what's inside!" she said.

Zach turned the shoe around so the opening was facing him. "Somebody's sock must have come off with their shoe," Zach said to his sister.

"I've done that plenty of times."

"I don't know why," Zoe said, "but somehow I think it's important."

Zach scrunched up his face. "A sock?" he said.

Zoe frowned. Maybe she was wrong. But something inside her said it had to do with the mystery. She didn't get to respond to her brother, because at that moment, Mr. Amaro poked his head in the door. He told them their dad was waiting for them outside the Bruins locker room.

Zach shrugged. "Out of time."

"Not yet," Zoe said. "This is just the end of regulation time. Remember, if Mike hadn't scored that goal at the end of Game 6, the Bruins and Sharks would have gone into overtime."

"So now we're in overtime?" Zach asked.

"Totally," said Zoe. "If Mike could find the net when he absolutely had to, we can find that necklace."

SIX

When they met their dad, Zach and Zoe asked him if there was any chance they could take one last look around the locker room. They would have to leave the arena soon, and the Bruins managers were due back from their coffee break any minute. Then they'd get to work on laundry and sharpening skates and making sure everything and everybody was ready for Game 7.

"If we can't find the necklace, maybe we

can at least find a clue," Zoe said to her dad.

"I'll ask," he said. "But I just want you both to remember that this is a very big room, and the necklace is a very small item."

"But, Dad," Zach said. "Don't you and mom always tell us to dream big?"

"All the time," he replied.

"And," Zoe said, "we're built a lot closer to the ground than the managers or anybody else. We might still be able to spot something they can't."

Danny Walker smiled.

"Every time I think I know how big your hearts are, you prove to me they've gotten even bigger," he said.

His friend from the Bruins, Mr. Greenberg, was still in the locker room. Mr. Greenberg said it was perfectly all right if the twins made one last search of the Bruins locker room before the managers got back.

Just as they had in the Lost and Found, Zach took one side of the room. Zoe took the other. They scanned the space almost the same way the Zamboni drove over the ice, walking up and down the room so as not to miss a thing. They went from locker to locker, thinking Mike might have walked over to one of his teammates after practice and forgot to mention it. Sometimes they got down on their hands and knees to look underneath the bench in front of the lockers. Then they'd switch sides, just on the chance that one of them had missed something, even though they hardly ever did.

Nothing.

"I just thought of something," Zoe said. "Mike's necklace is made of gold. Maybe if we dim the lights in here, the necklace will give off a little sparkle. That is, if it's even here, of course."

"You mean a little sparkle like the two of you give off?" Danny Walker said, pleased with his joke.

Mr. Greenberg dimmed the lights. Zach and Zoe spread out again, walking up and down in front of the lockers, then back to the middle of the carpeted room. Still nothing. Even Zach and Zoe Walker, who never gave up, were beginning to lose hope.

Zach was back on his hands and knees between Mike's locker and Alex Mozov's when he quietly said, "Oh boy, oh boy, oh boy."

He reached down underneath the chair closest to Alex's locker, then stood up and walked over to where his dad and Zoe were standing. He showed them the small gold clasp in the palm of his hand.

"Finally," Zach said to his dad and his sister, beaming. "A clue."

"A big clue," his sister said, "even for something so small. But it's still only a piece of the necklace."

"So where's the rest of it?" Zach asked, just as the lights in the locker room came back up.

SEVEN

It was the Bruins team managers, Tommy and Kevin, back from their brief coffee break. They were smiling at Zach and Zoe, who looked up, startled. It was as if they'd put the spotlight on them.

Tommy said, "I see our private detectives are still hard at work."

"Any progress?" Kevin asked.

Zach walked over and showed them both the clasp. He told them he and Zoe were sure it had to be part of Mike's necklace. Nothing else made sense.

"Well, none of us can give up now," Tommy said. "We all have to keep looking until we find that necklace. This has to be a total team effort."

"You sound like us," Zoe said to him.

The managers walked around the locker room, picking up towels and T-shirts and socks the players had left behind.

"Hockey players are about as neat as you are," Zoe said to Zach, giving him a little shove to show she was kidding.

While they were tidying up, the managers looked for the missing necklace at the same time. When their arms were full, they disappeared into the laundry room.

"I've got an idea," Zoe said.

"Another one?" said Zach.

"I have more than one per day," she said, playfully poking him with an elbow. "Follow me."

The twins followed Tommy and Kevin in the direction of the laundry room while their dad stayed behind with Mr. Greenberg. On the ride to the arena that morning, they'd thought the biggest excitement of their day would be getting inside the Bruins locker room. Now they were excited to be in a laundry room.

The surprises that began the day before when Grandpa Richie showed up at their house just kept coming. Starting with the size of the laundry room. The twins couldn't believe how big it was, with more washers and dryers than they'd ever seen in one place lined up against the far wall.

"Even though the big game tomorrow night is at the Garden," Tommy said, "some of the guys like to come over here in the morning to have a skate and loosen up. So we have to have all their practice gear washed and dried and ready for them."

"We even polish their skates," Kevin said.

"And," Tommy added, "we make sure the straps on every single helmet are fastened the way they're supposed to be."

Spread out on two long tables in the middle of the room were rows of helmets and skates and pads. Zach said to his sister that he felt as if they'd walked into a sporting goods store that sold only hockey equipment.

They'd already learned a lot today. Now they were also seeing how much work there was for Tommy and Kevin to do once practice was over. But despite all of Zach and Zoe's hard work so far, they still hadn't found Mike Gordon's necklace. And they knew they needed to find it soon. Because as supportive as their dad was being, they knew he wasn't going to let them spend the whole rest of the day at the Warrior Ice Arena.

"Your dad told us about some of the other mysteries the two of you have solved," Tommy said. "From missing baseballs to deflated footballs. He even told us you solved the mystery of who was fixing up your local basketball court."

Zoe puffed up her chest with pride. "But whenever we solve mysteries," she said, "we always appreciate a little help. And now we need a favor from you."

"Name it," Kevin said.

"Before you start washing things," Zoe said, "would you mind if we went through everything in here one more time?"

Tommy made a face.

"Going through the helmets and skates will be no problem," he said. "But the dirty laundry in that bin over there is kind of sweaty and gross."

Zoe grinned.

"I can handle it," she said. "And I know my brother can, too. He knows practically everything there is to know about sweaty, gross things."

"Hey!" Zach said.

That got a laugh out of Tommy and Kevin. They figured the best thing for them to do was gather all of Mike's gear and put it on one of the side tables. So they moved some of the other equipment aside, and laid out Mike's T-shirt, pants, jersey, socks, skates, helmet, and pads.

Zoe stared at all of it.

"Did you spot a clue?" Zach asked.

"No," she said, shaking her head. "But I'm starting to think I might have spotted one a little while ago without realizing it."

"Now you're the one being mysterious," Zach said. "And we're running out of time."

"That means it really is time for us to get lucky," his sister said.

Zoe scrunched her face as she picked up Mike's sweaty socks and T-shirt. She turned the shirt inside out. Then it was time for her to reach inside the socks.

"Eeeew," she said.

"Big eeeew," her brother said. "But you said you were ready for this."

"Maybe not quite as ready as I thought," she said, pinching her nose.

But the necklace wasn't inside the socks, and it wasn't inside his skates, either. Mike said he had checked them, but Zach and Zoe looked again, just to be sure. Now they did feel as if the clock was running out on them. From the locker room they heard their dad yell out, "Twooooooooo minutes," the way the announcer did when there were two minutes left in a game.

The last thing for them to check was Mike's helmet.

"This feels like our last chance," Zach said.

They took a deep breath while Zoe carefully turned the helmet over. She was surprised at how much padding was inside, even though hockey helmets appeared to be about half the size of the ones football players wore.

Zoe and Zach let out a collective sigh. Nothing fell out of the helmet when Zoe turned it over. But she wasn't done yet.

Zoe closed her eyes for just a moment. Dream big, their dad said. She was doing that now, trying to imagine the end of the story she and Zach wanted. Then she stuck her head closer to the inside of the helmet.

The padding was dark, which would make it easier to see the gold of Mike Gordon's necklace if it was there.

Suddenly, something caught her eye. It was small, but there was no mistaking it.

A glittering piece of gold chain was sticking out from the padding. When Zoe pulled on it, the locket appeared. It was opened to show the picture of Mike's wife and children inside.

EIGHT

As excited and happy as Zoe was, she was careful taking out the necklace. It was already broken and she didn't want to cause any more damage.

Zach had already yelled for his dad to come join them. Tommy and Kevin high-fived each other.

"Why were you so sure that the necklace was stuck in his gear somewhere?" Zach asked his sister.

"It was partly because Mike had told us how distracted he'd been about Game 7," Zoe said. "But more than that, it was seeing the sock stuck inside that shoe in the Lost and Found."

"But the necklace wasn't in Mike's socks," Zach said. "Or his skates."

"It was more about how the sock ended up in the shoe," Zoe said. "When someone pulled their shoe off, their sock came with it. I thought maybe the necklace had gotten stuck in Mike's helmet the same way."

Zach nodded. "Like when he took off his helmet, the necklace might have slipped off at the same time."

"And that's how it broke," Zoe completed the thought. "When Mike pulled his helmet off, the necklace came with it. But it was too small to fit over his head, so the clasp came loose."

"That's how the clasp must have ended up on the floor," said Zach. "The rest of the neck-lace got stuck in his helmet."

"Exactly," Zoe said.

Zach smiled and gave his sister a high five.

"But our work still isn't done," Zoe added. "Now we have to fix the necklace."

"But shouldn't we have somebody call Mike and tell him we found it?" Zach said.

"Good luck with that," Kevin said. "Mike isn't just superstitious about that necklace. From now until he gets to the Garden tomorrow, he'll have his phone turned off, won't check his email, and refuses to look at social media. His wife does the same. He just wants quiet time at home with his family."

"Even better!" Zoe said. "We can get the necklace fixed, so when he does get it back, it'll be as good as new."

"Can you get it fixed by game time?" Kevin asked.

He saw Zach and Zoe grinning at each other, then up at their dad.

"We can," Zoe said with confidence.

Zach shared his sister's excitement. "We know somebody who can do it."

"A jeweler?" Kevin asked.

"Our mom," Zach and Zoe said together.

"She'll know how?" said Tommy.

Zach grinned. "She pretty much knows everything."

NINE

Their dad drove them all back to Middletown. When they got home, the twins jumped out of the car and raced inside to tell their mom about the mystery of the lost necklace. They recounted every detail of their search, including how they found it.

"Whoa, whoa, whoa!" Tess said. "Slow down!" She was sitting at the kitchen table. The twins were obviously excited and took turns telling their mom the rest of the story.

"Mike will be so happy to get his locket back in time for Game 7," Zach said. "It was our lucky day and even luckier that we have a master jeweler in our family."

"Master jeweler?" Tess Walker said. "And who might that be?"

"You!" the two of them shouted in one voice.

The Walker twins admired both their parents for different reasons. They knew how great their dad had been in the NBA and now, as a popular television personality. Even what a good coach he was whenever he coached one of their teams. But their mom was really something, too. She could paint. She could write. She could cook like a master chef on television.

And in her spare time, she even made some of her own jewelry. The twins often wondered how she found the time, on top of everything she already did to be the world's greatest mom.

"Let's have a look at this very famous necklace," she said.

Zoe carefully lifted it out of the small box the Bruins managers had given her. Tess Walker took it from Zoe and held it up to the light. She could see where the chain had broken and Zach produced the clasp he'd found on the locker room floor.

Tess smiled.

"Fixing this will be easier than scoring on an empty net," she said. "All we have to do is reattach the clasp to the chain."

Zach and Zoe beamed. They knew their mom could fix the necklace. There was no way this day could get any better.

Just then, Tess turned to her husband. "By the way," she said, "do you think we should tell them the last surprise?"

"There's more?" Zoe said in disbelief.

"Just one more," their dad promised.

"Tell us!" the twins begged.

"Well," he said, "you know we'll all be going to Game 7 tomorrow night, and I'm getting in early with my media pass."

"That's when you'll give Mike his necklace, right?" Zoe said.

"No," their dad said. "That's when the two of you can give him his necklace."

He reached into his jacket then, and produced two Boston Bruins all-access passes Mr. Greenberg had given him after Zach and Zoe found the necklace.

"You're going to visit one more locker room," Danny Walker said to the twins. "The real one this time."

There was only one thing for the twins to do then. They jumped and spun and bumped elbows and knees—their special high five reserved for only the most special occasions.

Then their parents joined in. It was one more team effort. And in that moment, the Walker family didn't need the necklace in Tess's hand to feel lucky.

TEN

Another game day superstition Mike Gordon had was that he always showed up at the locker room exactly three hours before the puck dropped. Game 7 was scheduled to start at eight o'clock. So at five o'clock sharp, Danny Walker took Zach and Zoe through the locker room door and over to where Mike was sitting in front of his changing area. Neither one of the twins could believe they were in this locker room, the real one, this close to Game 7.

Their dad always said that sports were about making memories. Now they were about to make another one, for themselves, and for Mike Gordon.

They didn't waste any time.

"We found your necklace," Zoe said, holding up the locket for Mike to see.

"No way!" Mike Gordon said. "I thought it was gone for good."

"Think of us as your own personal Lost and Found," Zach said, winking at Zoe.

Zoe handed Mike the necklace as if she were presenting him a priceless piece of gold, which to him it probably was. Mike reached around his neck to put it on.

"How did you find it?" he finally asked, unable to wipe the smile off his face.

"Kind of a long story," Zoe replied.

Mike raised his eyebrows. "We do have three hours."

Zach and Zoe told him everything that

happened after he left the locker room. How the necklace must have come off when he removed his helmet after practice ended.

"You never gave up," Mike said.

"You never do on the ice," Zach said right back.

Mike reached out and shook Zach's hand. Then he did the same with Zoe. He looked up at Danny Walker and said, "You've got a couple of pretty amazing kids here."

"They certainly keep amazing their mother and me," Danny said, placing a hand on each twin's shoulder.

"How can I possibly thank you enough?" Mike said to the twins.

"Easy," Zoe said. "Go out there and win the Stanley Cup!"

Not only did Tess Walker and the twins have great seats at the arena, but they saw a great game, too. The Bruins and Sharks were tied at 3–3 by the end of the final period. It looked as if the teams were about to go into a second overtime, which the twins didn't think they could handle. It was too much excitement! But suddenly, Mike stole the puck from a Sharks defenseman, went in against their goalie on a breakaway, and scored the backhand goal that won Game 7 for the Bruins.

Zach and Zoe and their mom watched the celebration on the ice. Then the two teams got into a handshake line, the same as the twins did after one of their games. They all watched as two men wearing white gloves came walking down the red carpet that had been rolled out onto the ice. They were carrying the Stanley Cup. By then it had been announced to the crowd that Mike Gordon had been voted the MVP of the finals.

After his speech, the NHL commissioner handed the Stanley Cup to Mike, who held it high in the air and began skating around the ice with it. His teammates took their turns doing the same.

And just when the Walker twins thought

their night couldn't get any better, it did.

An hour after the game ended, when their dad had finished doing all of his television work, he met Zach, Zoe, and their mom at the media lounge.

"You all need to come with me right away," he said.

"Where?" Zoe asked.

"Mystery," was all their dad said.

He walked them all down a long hallway and into a tiny room next to the Bruins locker room.

Waiting for them inside was Mike Gordon.

So was the Stanley Cup.

"I figured my two new good-luck charms should get to do what I just did on the ice," Mike said.

"What's that?" Zach asked.

"Hold up the Stanley Cup," Mike replied, like it was obvious.

Zoe's eyes went wide. "Won't it be too heavy?"

"I'll help you," Mike said. "The way you helped me."

Then they all lifted the Stanley Cup together.

Team effort.

JOIN THE TEAM.
SOLVE THE CASE!

Read all the Zach & Zoe Mysteries

31901065556724